A NOODLE
UP YOUR NOSE

A NOODLE UP YOUR NOSE

Frieda Wishinsky

with illustrations by
Louise-Andrée Laliberté

ORCA BOOK PUBLISHERS

National Library of Canada Cataloguing in Publication Data

Wishinsky, Frieda

A noodle up your nose / Frieda Wishinsky; with illustrations by

Louise-Andrée Laliberté.

(Orca echoes)

ISBN 1-55143-294-3

I. Laliberté, Louise-Andrée II. Title. III. Series.

PS8595.I834N66 2004   jC813'.54   C2004-900641-x

Library of Congress Control Number: 2004100824

Summary: When Violet thinks that she isn't invited to Kate's birthday party,
she spreads rumors that threaten to ruin everything.

Teachers' guide available from Orca Book Publishers.

Orca Book Publishers gratefully acknowledges the support
of its publishing program provided by the following
agencies: the Department of Canadian Heritage, the Canada
Council for the Arts, and the British Columbia Arts Council.

Design by Lynn O'Rourke
Printed and bound in Canada

Orca Book Publishers
1030 North Park Street
Victoria, BC Canada
V8T 1C6

Orca Book Publishers
PO Box 468
Custer, WA USA
98240-0468

07 06 05 04 • 4 3 2 1

For my friend Norene Gilletz
who really knows her noodles.
—F.W.

Chapter One
Kate M'Mate

"Only twenty more days till my birthday!" sang Kate Morris, jumping up and down on her bed. "Only twenty more days till I'm seven!"

Kate flopped down on her stomach.

Seven was her lucky number. Seven was the year she was going to learn how to ride a two-wheeler, swim in the deep end and rollerblade down her street. Her best friend, Jake promised he'd help her learn. He was seven-and-a-half and could do all those things already.

Kate was glad she was having a party this year. Last year she had the flu on her birthday. Then her mom and dad had the flu. No one could visit them for two weeks. But this year she was going to have the best party.

The only trouble was it was going to be too big. Her parents insisted she invite her whole class.

"I can't invite Leo," Kate had protested. "He shoots spitballs into my hair at recess."

"I'll make sure he doesn't spit anything in our house," said her dad, but her dad didn't know how sneaky Leo could be.

"I can't invite Brad," said Kate. "His nose is always runny, and he wipes the goop on his sleeve."

"I'll make sure we have plenty of tissues," said Kate's mom.

"I can't invite Violet," said Kate. "She's so bossy, she always wants everyone to do everything her way."

"Just boss her back," said Kate's dad.

Kate sighed. That was easy for her dad to say. No one could boss Violet back. Violet always got her way.

At least Jake would be at her party. Kate smiled when she thought about how his curly red hair looked like a tangled forest even after he combed it. She thought about how before any adventure, he'd say, "Come on Kate M'Mate," like they were pirates.

So who cared if spitball Leo, drippy-nosed Brad and bossy-mouth Violet came to her party? It would still be fun as long as Jake was there.

Chapter Two
Late Jake

The first person to greet Kate at school the next morning was Violet. She cornered Kate near the coat hooks.

"Are you having a party this year?" Violet asked, brushing her long blonde hair. Violet was always brushing her hair. Before Kate could answer, Violet burbled on. "My party is in November and it's going to be amazing. My mom's hiring the best magician in town, Magic Merlin. She's ordering a three-tiered birthday cake from Cake Delight, the best bakery in the world. And wait till you see the gorgeous dress I'm getting from

Fun Frocks, that new store that sells the cutest stuff. Oh, there's Lila. Gotta go."

And with that, Violet buzzed off to brag about her amazing birthday party to Lila.

Kate was glad she didn't have to discuss her party with Violet. She wasn't having Magic Merlin entertain at her party. She and her mom were baking her birthday cake together. And she hated dresses, so she wasn't going to wear one, even on her birthday. But she was going to wear great socks. They were red and black stripes. Perfect for a pirate.

Maybe she'd even wear her red shirt and black pants and pull her straight brown hair back into a ponytail. Maybe she'd cover her eye with a black patch and borrow her mom's red scarf to wear as a sash. Maybe she'd have a pirate party!

Kate was so busy dreaming about her party that she didn't hear the first bell ring.

"Kate, hurry!" called Jake, zooming past her into his seat.

Kate raced into her seat just as the second bell clanged.

"Phew! I was almost late. My alarm clock forgot to ring," said Jake.

Kate laughed. "Your alarm clock can't forget. It's not alive," she said.

"It is alive," said Jake with a straight face. "It wants me to be late."

"Oh sure," said Kate.

Jake was famous for being late. He was also famous for his reasons for being late. Last year in grade one, he told the teacher that he was late because his goldfish died. The trouble was that Jake didn't have a goldfish.

The real problem was that Jake loved to sleep in the morning. His mother said that waking him up was like trying to wake up a rock. Jake didn't hear her say, "Good morning." He didn't hear her say, "Get up, Jake." He didn't even hear her shout, "Hurry! It's late, Jake!"

Last week his mother bought him an alarm clock, but that didn't seem to be helping much either.

This morning, Jake wasn't the only one who was late. Mr. Bolin, their new teacher, dashed into the room five minutes after the bell.

"Sorry, class," he said, huffing and puffing. "My alarm clock didn't go off this morning. I don't understand it. I'm sure I set it last night."

Jake nudged Kate in the arm. "See," he said. "His alarm clock is alive too."

Chapter Three
Pirate Plans

At recess, Violet skipped over to Kate.

"I hear you're having a birthday party soon. Are you having clowns? Clowns are so much fun," said Violet.

"No," said Kate.

"Oh," said Violet, turning her nose up. "Then what ARE you doing at your party?"

"Well...I..." Kate began.

Before Kate could finish her sentence, Violet turned her back and shouted, "Hey Lila. Wait up!" Then she ran off.

Kate plunked down on a swing and pumped.

Violet made her so mad. She always asked questions and never waited for answers.

Up. Down. Up. Down. Kate bent her knees and arms. The swing flew higher and higher.

Where was Jake? He'd gone to the bathroom before recess, but he promised he'd meet her at the swings.

"Hey, Kate M'Mate," rumbled a voice. It was Jake. He was standing behind her and pushing her swing! Kate didn't dare turn around to look at him. She knew she'd fall off the swing if she did.

Suddenly the girl in the next swing hopped off and Jake hopped on. Side by side they rose higher and higher. She felt like they were acrobats flying through air. She felt like they were jets criss-crossing the sky. She felt like they were birds gliding above the trees. She wished they could swing forever.

Then the bell rang. Together they jumped off the swings.

"Jake," said Kate, as they walked back to class. "I'm going to ask my mom if I can have a pirate party."

"Hey. That's neat. You could ask everyone to dress up like a pirate," he suggested.

"And we could bake a red and black strawberry chocolate cake," said Kate.

"And you could get red and black jelly beans," said Jake.

"I'll ask my mom today," said Kate, as they slipped into their seats.

Kate didn't wait long. The minute her mom picked her up after school, she said, "Can I have a pirate birthday party?"

"That's an unusual idea for a birthday party," said her mom.

"It will be so much fun," said Kate. "We can make a pirate cake and blow up red and black balloons and hunt for buried treasure and play pin the fin on the shark and…"

"Hold on, pirate girl," said Kate's mom, laughing. "You've convinced me."

"Oh, thank you! Thank you!" said Kate, hugging her mom tight. "You're the best mom in the world. And can I borrow your red scarf to wear as a sash, please?"

"Why not?" said her mom.

"Yippee!" sang Kate, dancing up and down the sidewalk. "I have to tell Jake."

As soon as they arrived home, Kate ran to the phone.

"Kate M'Mate, it's going to be great," sang Jake.

"Don't forget, you can't be late," sang Kate.

"Me? Late?" said Jake. "Never. Well, never for a party!"

Chapter Four
Imagine

"Slow down, Kate," said her mom the next day after school. "I can't keep up with your ideas."

"But imagine if we turned the basement into a pirate island. We could make the couch a pirate ship and the rug the ocean and the coffee table could be the plank the prisoners have to walk across before they fall into the ocean."

"I don't think I want twenty kids bouncing on our couch, jumping off our table and drowning on our rug," said Kate's mother. "So let's just have pirate food, pirate games and pirate decorations."

"But, Mom. Just imagine…" Kate began. Then she saw the stern look on her mom's face. "Okay," she said. "No island, but we have to make pirate patches. Everyone has to get a patch to decorate."

"Sounds good," said her mom. "Let's go shopping this weekend for birthday supplies."

"Then I'll write up all the invitations and give them out on Monday," said Kate.

For the rest of that week, Kate couldn't wait for the weekend. She couldn't stop herself from dreaming up more ideas for the party.

Her mom didn't like most of them.

"Kate," said her mom. "I'm afraid someone would choke if we buried treasure in the birthday cake. And no duels, especially not with broomsticks."

"What if we buried treasure in a bucket of sand?" asked Kate. "We have lots of sand in the sandbox. And what if we had duels with chopsticks or even Popsicle sticks? What if…"

"Kate, please," said her mom. "No more ideas. We can't do everything. It's a three-hour party. Not a week long festival."

"I just want everyone to have fun," said Kate.

"If we do all the things you've thought of, everyone will be too exhausted to have fun. Especially your parents."

Chapter Five
The Party Store

On Saturday morning, Kate and her mom drove to The Party Store at the mall.

It didn't take long to find red and black balloons and streamers. They even found black eye patches and sparkly pirate stickers to decorate them. But Kate couldn't find pirate invitations anywhere.

"There's nothing here for a pirate party," she told her mom after looking at dozens of invitations. "All the invitations have dolls, cowboys, baseballs or clowns on them."

"Maybe you should make up your own invitations," suggested her mom.

24

"Yes!" said Kate. "I could draw pirates, parrots, buried treasure and sailing ships."

"Good idea," said her mom. "Now, let's pay for the decorations and stickers."

As they waited in line, someone tapped Kate on her shoulder.

She spun around. It was Violet with Lila and Lila's mother.

"Are you shopping for your party?" asked Violet.

"Yes," said Kate.

"Why do you have pirate stickers?" asked Lila. "Do you like pirates?"

"Yes," said Kate. "I'm having a pirate party for my birthday."

"You are?" said Violet, nudging Lila in the side and making a face. Then they both giggled as if Kate had said the stupidest thing in the world.

"Are you going to have pirate food like snakes, worms and shark guts at your party?" asked Violet.

"No. Pirates don't eat that stuff," said Kate.

"I bet they do," sneered Violet. Then Violet strutted out of the store with Lila and Lila's mother.

Kate turned to her mother. "See what I mean about Violet?" said Kate. "She always thinks she knows everything. She always thinks everyone likes what she likes. She always thinks what she likes is the best. I wish I didn't have to invite her to my party."

"You have to invite her, Kate," said Kate's mom. "You can't leave just one person out."

"I know I can't," said Kate, "but I wish I could."

Chapter Six
Each One Different

"Look, Mom!" said Kate. "I'm making each one different." Kate held up an invitation with a parrot perched on a pirate's head. "Can you help me write the words?"

"Sure," said Kate's mom.

Kate's mom helped her write COME AS A PIRATE TO KATE'S PIRATE PARTY. Kate carefully copied the words on the balloon popping out of the parrot's mouth.

"That's great," said her mom, "but are you sure you want to make each invitation different? That's a lot of work. You could make one drawing and we could photocopy it nineteen times."

"But I love drawing" said Kate. "I don't want everyone to have the same picture on their invitation."

Kate sat at the kitchen table and worked all Saturday afternoon on her invitations. By four o'clock she'd finished ten. She'd made an invitation of a pirate digging for treasure on a deserted island. She'd made an invitation of a pirate riding a whale. She'd made an invitation of a one-legged pirate dancing across the deck of his ship.

"I'm so tired. My hand feels like it's going to fall off!" Kate said.

"Why don't you take a hot chocolate break?" suggested her mom.

"A hot chocolate break with whipped cream, please?" asked Kate, popping her head up.

"Why not?" said her mom and she began to get the hot chocolate ready.

As Kate and her mom sipped their drinks, the phone rang. It was Jake.

"Want to play tomorrow?" he asked.

"After I finish nine more pirate invitations. I'm drawing each one with a different picture," Kate explained.

"Want some help?" asked Jake.

"Hey! That would be great," said Kate. "You draw terrific pirates. Come over in the morning."

The next morning at ten, Jake's dad dropped him off at Kate's house. Kate showed Jake her ten finished invitations.

"I love this one where the pirate catches a shoe instead of a fish," said Jake.

"Look at this one where the pirate catches a sea monster with nine green arms and one green eyeball," sad Kate.

"That gives me an idea," said Jake and he picked up a pencil and began to sketch. He drew a pirate swinging a fishing line across the ship and catching another pirate by the pants.

By one o'clock, Jake had made four invitations and Kate had made five. One was for Jake. They were finished!

"I love this one," said Kate's mom to Jake. Jake's invitation showed a pirate opening a treasure chest full of toilet paper. "He doesn't look happy."

"He wanted to find gold," said Jake.

"Sometimes toilet paper is better than gold," said Kate.

Chapter Seven
Excuses, Excuses, Excuses

The next morning Kate was up early. She carefully placed each of her nineteen party invitations into an envelope. On each envelope she wrote a person's name in red and black marker.

"I love my party already," she told her mother, dancing around the kitchen. "I hope everyone comes."

"Everyone?" said her mother. "Even Violet?"

"Even Violet and Leo and Brad. I feel so happy that nothing any of them do or say is going to bother me," said Kate.

Kate's mom grabbed her jacket and purse.

"That's the spirit, my pirate girl! Let's go so you can hand out those invitations before class," she said.

Kate and her mom hurried out the door.

There were only three kids in class when Kate arrived, and they were playing with Roland the gerbil at the back. Kate slipped an invitation into everyone's desk. Then she joined the kids at the back with Roland.

The bell rang. Kate zoomed to her desk. As she did, she glanced at Jake's seat. It was empty.

Mr. Bolin walked into class. "Good morning, class," he said, as Jake dashed into his seat. "And good morning, Jake. Did you have a little trouble getting up again?"

"It wasn't me," said Jake. "My dad brought me to school this morning and just as we were about to go out the door, he saw that he forgot his keys. So he had to run upstairs and look through five pairs of pants pockets till he found them. That's why I'm late."

Jake smiled at Mr. Bolin.

Mr. Bolin did not smile back. "That's a good story, Jake," he said. "Even a possible story, but it would be much more believable if it wasn't your seventh late excuse this year, and it's only October. There was the sudden-grandmother-visit excuse. The no-clean-socks excuse. The cat-at-the-vet excuse. The stomachache, headache and nosebleed excuses. And my all time favorite—the itchy toes excuse."

"But my toes really did itch, Mr. Bolin," Jake protested.

"I'm sure they did, Jake. It's not the reasons you're late, it's how often you're late. See if you can arrive on time from now on. Otherwise, I may have to send you to have a little chat with the principal about all your excuses."

"I'll try, Mr. Bolin. I really will. I like your class," said Jake, flashing Mr. Bolin a big smile.

This time Mr. Bolin smiled back. "Despite everything, Jake, I like having you in it too," he said.

Chapter Eight
Goop and Guts

The rumors about Kate's party began at recess.

"Did you hear?" said Leo. "Kate's serving radish pie at her party."

"Did you hear?" said Ben. "Kate's serving spinach juice at her party."

"Did you hear?" said Lila, "Kate's serving garlic cupcakes at her party."

"It's not true," Kate told them.

"Well, that's what we heard," said Lila.

"Who told you that?" asked Kate.

"I don't remember," said Lila in a huffy voice. "I just know that's what I heard."

"Was it Violet?" asked Kate.

"I told you. I don't remember," snarled Lila.

"Well, I'm not having radish pie, spinach juice or garlic cupcakes at my party. I'm having strawberry and chocolate pirate cake and it's going to be delicious," said Kate.

"Pirate cake?" said Lila. "How can pirate cake be delicious? Pirates eat goop and guts."

"They do not," said Kate.

"Do too. Do too. Do too," said Lila. Then she stuck out her tongue and ran off.

Kate ran to the swings where Jake was waiting for her. "Hey," he said. "What took you so long? It's not easy reserving a swing. Two girls almost beat me up for it. I had to tell them that you had an emergency phone call from home and would be back in a second."

"Jake, why did you say that?" said Kate. "Now everyone is going to ask me what happened. You know how stories get spread." Then Kate told Jake about the rumors about her party.

"I bet it was Violet," he said. "She can be mean for no good reason. One day she told me that I had a hole in my pants and I didn't."

"Well, I'm going to ask her at lunch," said Kate. "But I don't understand. I invited her to my party. Why does she have to be mean?"

"Maybe it's something she ate. You know how my mom tells me not to eat too much sugar because it makes me hyper? Well, maybe if you eat certain foods too much, you get mean."

"That's crazy," said Kate, laughing.

"But who knows," said Jake. "It might be true."

"Maybe it's broccoli," said Kate. "Every time my mom makes me eat it, I feel sick. And when I feel sick, I feel angry. And when I feel angry, I feel mean. Maybe Violet eats too much broccoli." Kate laughed at the thought of Violet's face stuffed with broccoli.

"Yes," said Jake as they walked back to class. "Broccoli could be it."

Chapter Nine
Seaweed and Slugs

Kate confronted Violet at lunch. "Was it you?" she said.

"Was it me what?" said Violet, brushing her hair at her desk.

"Did you spread rumors about my party?" asked Kate.

"I don't spread rumors," said Violet, rolling her green eyes.

"Well, everything is going to be delicious at my party," said Kate. "It's going to be a great party."

"Really," said Violet in a voice that made Kate know Violet didn't believe a word. Violet turned her

39

back on Kate. "Lila, over here," she called. "Bring your lunch and sit with me."

Kate walked away. How could she make people believe that the rumors about her party weren't true?

All the way home, Kate wondered what she could do to stop the rumors, but she couldn't think of anything. Would the kids really believe the rumors? Would they still come to her party, no matter what crazy stories they heard?

But as soon as she reached school the next morning, Kate heard new rumors.

"Did you hear?" said Alice. "Kate's making someone wash all the dishes at her party."

"Did you hear?" said Andrew. "Kate's making someone eat spider legs at her party."

"Did you hear?" said Charlene. "Kate's making someone stick a noodle up his nose at her party."

Kate ran around all recess telling people that the rumors weren't true. But it was like plugging a hole

in a dam. She stopped one rumor and another one popped out of nowhere.

By lunchtime, there were newer, crazier rumors.

There were rumors that Kate was decorating her house with spider webs and anthills.

There were rumors that the loot bags would be filled with seaweed and slugs.

There were rumors that everyone had to eat a worm before Kate would let them eat cake.

"Ugh," screeched Alice. "That is so gross."

"It's a big gross lie," said Kate. "Who's making all these stories up?"

But Alice didn't know, and no one else did either.

"Oh Jake," said Kate on the phone that night. "What if no one comes to my party on Sunday?"

"I'll be there," said Jake.

"Thanks, Jake. You're a good friend, but a party needs lots of people. What if it's just you and me at my party? Who'll eat all the cake? How can we play games with only two people?"

42

Kate's mom and dad tried to reassure her that no one really believed silly rumors, but Kate still wasn't confident that anyone would come to her party.

After supper, Kate and her mom filled the loot bags with chocolate coins, gummy fish, candy jewelry and Find the Treasure puzzles. For awhile, Kate was having so much fun, she forgot to worry about her party.

But when Kate and her mom looked around the basement to find the perfect spot to hide the cardboard crocodile they'd made for Hunt the Croc, Kate burst into tears. "What if no one's here to find the croc? What if…"

"Oh, Kate," said her mom. "Let's just have fun preparing for the party. Everything will work out. You'll see."

Kate wiped her tears. "I know it's Violet, Mom. I'm going to find out the truth tomorrow. She can't spoil my party for no reason. It's not fair."

The next day, Violet was out in the morning at the dentist. She came back to school after lunch. Kate had to wait till the end of the day to talk to her.

Kate's knees shook as she walked over to Violet. Violet was talking to Lila. Kate took a deep breath. "I want to talk to you," she told Violet in a firm voice.

"I don't want to talk to you," said Violet, turning her back on Kate. "I'm busy and I'm going home."

But Kate wouldn't let Violet stop her.

"Why are you trying to ruin my party?" she asked. "I didn't do anything to you."

Violet spun around. "Oh, yes, you did," she barked, waving her finger in front of Kate's face. "You didn't invite me to your stupid party."

"I did too," said Kate. "I put everyone's invitation in their desk. Look in your desk and you'll find it."

"There's nothing there," said Violet, glancing quickly in her desk.

"Look again," said Kate. "I put the invitation there. If you don't believe me, ask my mom."

This time Violet bent over and peered inside her desk. She pulled out a pile of crumpled paper, three nibbled pencils, a long, tattered hair ribbon and a squished tuna sandwich.

"See? Your stupid invitation is not here," she said.

"Look again," insisted Kate. "There's more stuff in your desk."

Violet yanked out a handful of green and pink socks, a crushed paper bag and a crumpled piece of paper. The paper was smeared with tuna and mayonnaise and had a picture of a smiling parrot. It said, Come as a Pirate to Kate's Pirate Party.

"Oh…" stammered Violet. "I guess you did invite me to your party. Well…That's great. See you on Sunday."

And with that, Violet ran out the door.

Kate looked around the room. The classroom was almost empty. All the kids had gone home except for Brad, who was pulling a wad of crumpled tissues out of his desk and stuffing them into his schoolbag.

Kate sighed. Now she knew why Violet had spread the rumors. Violet thought Kate hadn't invited her to her party. But so what if Kate knew the truth now? The damage was done. Violet wouldn't tell anyone the truth. That would make her look like a liar.

"Hurry, Kate," Jake called from the front of the room. "My mom's waiting outside. Remember, she's going to drive you home today."

Kate trudged out to join Jake. She pictured Violet coming to her party.

Kate shivered. It was a terrible thought.

"Oh, Mom, the cake is beautiful!" said Kate as her mom placed the iced chocolate cake on the counter. It had a layer of strawberry jam in the middle.

"Now you can decorate it," said Kate's mom, handing Kate a bag of red and black jellybeans.

Kate made a pattern around the edge of the cake. In the center of the cake, she used the jellybeans to make a pirate face with a crooked smile.

Her mom piped a strawberry icing pirate's hat on the pirate's head. She piped seven small red flowers inside the hat.

48

"Perfect!" exclaimed Kate.

"Now, let's set the table," said her mom. Kate and her mom placed twenty red paper plates on the two large tables they'd set up in the basement. Beside them they placed black napkins and black paper cups. Kate's dad blew up twenty red and black balloons and hung them around the room.

"Why don't you get into your pirate outfit," suggested her mom. "Your friends should be here in half an hour."

Kate's stomach knotted as she raced upstairs. All weekend, she'd tried not to worry about who would come to her party, but every once in a while a worry crept into her head. Now the party was only half an hour away. Please come, everybody, she prayed. Please come.

Kate slipped into her black pants and red shirt. She wrapped her mom's red scarf around her waist. As she tied the red bandanna around her head, the bell rang. Who could that be? Her party didn't start till 2:00 and it was only 1:30.

"Kate, you have a guest," called her mom.

Kate stuck her black eye patch over her left eye and raced down the stairs.

It was Violet. She was dressed in black pants, a shimmery black shirt and a red sash.

"Hi," said Kate "You're early. My party doesn't officially start till 2:00."

"Oh, that's okay," said Violet. "The invitation was smeared and I couldn't read the time right.

Lila can't come. She has the flu. Here's your present."

Violet stuck a long narrow box into Kate's hand.

"Thanks," said Kate.

"Do you like my pirate outfit?" asked Violet, twirling around. "The sash is real silk. It's my mother's and it cost so much, you wouldn't believe it."

"It's pretty," said Kate.

"So, where's the party gonna be?"

"In my basement," said Kate.

"I hate basements. Basements are creepy!"

Despite Violet's groans, she followed Kate down the stairs to the basement.

"This isn't too bad," said Violet. She looked up and down the basement like an exterminator hunting for roaches. "Your furniture is pretty old, but at least it doesn't smell. My Aunt Carol's basement smells like dead bodies. I like the balloons, and your cake is great. Where did you buy it?"

"I didn't. My mom and I made it."

"Wow. That's pretty good. What flavor is it?"

"Strawberry and chocolate," said Kate.

"I love strawberry. Can I have two roses? I love cake roses."

"I don't know. There are only seven and someone else might want a rose."

"But I came early, and anyway, why isn't anyone else here yet? Are you sure anyone is coming to your party besides me?"

Kate bit her lip. She wanted to scream at Violet that if no one came to the party, it was all Violet's fault. But Kate couldn't say that.

"It's still a little before 2:00," she said instead. "Everyone else will be here soon."

"Well, I hope so," said Violet. "It will be a very boring party if it's just you and me."

Chapter Eleven
Party!

"It's ten after two," announced Violet, tapping her fingers on the table. Tap. Tap. Tap. "And no one's here. No one's coming to your party but me."

"Jake is coming," Kate insisted. "I know he is."

"If he comes," said Violet, laughing, "it will probably be at midnight. He's never on time for anything. Let's cut that cake so this party isn't a total waste. I want three roses. No one else is here to eat them anyway."

"I'm not cutting the cake," said Kate firmly. "And if no one comes to my party, it's your fault. You spread those rumors about my party."

"Big deal," said Violet, tapping her fingers again. "If the kids liked you, they'd come anyway."

A lump started in Kate's throat. Don't cry, she told herself. Violet is just saying those things to make you cry. Kate choked the lump down.

The two girls glared at each other.

"This is the worst party I've ever been to," said Violet. "Cut that cake now or I'm going home."

Kate stood up. "No," she said. "I won't cut it."

Violet stood up. "Then I'm calling my mother to pick me up right now. I hate your party, Kate. It's stupid and boring and dumb."

"Call her then," said Kate, and she handed Violet the phone.

For an instant, Violet hesitated. Then she grabbed the phone from Kate and dialed. "Mom," said Violet loudly, "you have to pick me up NOW. I'm not staying another minute at this stupid party. If I stay another minute, I will throw up."

Five minutes later, Violet opened the door to leave.

"Do you want your present back?" asked Kate.

"No," said Violet. "Keep it. It's just a stupid game. I don't even like it. I got two for my birthday, so I gave you one."

And with that, Violet flounced out of Kate's house.

Kate ran up the stairs to her room and threw herself on her bed. The clock beside her bed said 2:16.

No one is coming, she thought. Violet is right. Even Jake isn't coming.

Kate stared as the minutes ticked by:

2:17

2:18

2:19

Kate slammed the clock face down on the table. She yanked off her eye patch. Tears dribbled down her face. She stood up to undo her pirate sash.

"Kate!" her mom called up the stairs. "Come down. You have guests!"

Guests? Kate wiped her eyes. She straightened her shirt, tightened her sash and stuck her patch

back up on her left eye. Then she ran downstairs. Her heart beat hard at each step. Yes. She could hear voices! Was Jake here?

The voices grew louder as Kate headed down to the basement. There weren't just one or two voices. There was a whole class of voices!

Kate opened the door to the basement. A roomful of smiling faces greeted her. "Happy Birthday!" they sang.

Kate felt like her heart would burst as she looked at the decorations, the food, the presents, her family and all her friends.

Jake was smiling his goofiest, friendliest smile and wearing baggy black pants and a red vest. Alice, Andrew, Charlene, Ben and Carla were all dressed up like pirates. Even Leo was smiling, and Brad's nose was as dry as a cactus.

"Sorry we're late," said Jake. "I know I said I'd never be late for your party, but I really have a good excuse this time."

"He does," said Andrew. "He told us that Violet spread all those rumors because she thought she wasn't invited to your party. So we all decided to surprise you and come to your party together. We started out early, but my dad had a flat tire on the way."

"And it took twenty minutes to fix," said Alice.

"But here we are, Kate M'Mate," said Jake.

Kate's eyes glowed as bright as her candles. "Thank you all," she said. "This is the best party ever. And you all are the best mates a pirate could ever have."

Frieda Wishinsky is the award-winning author of many popular books for children, including *Just Call Me Joe* (Orca, 2003) and *Each One Special* (Orca, 1998). Frieda lives in Toronto with her husband and family.

Other books in the Orca Echoes Series

The Birthday Girl
by Jean Little
illustrated by June Lawrason

Down the Chimney
with Googol and Googolplex
by Nelly Kazenbroot

Louise-Andrée Laliberté has built a career as an artist, illustrator, and graphic designer, Her books include the popular french series of more than thiretten books *Noémie*. *Hank and Fergus* is her most recent picture book. She recieved the CAPIC's Gold Prize for book illustration for her work in *L'Homme Étoile* She lives with her family and her big black dog in Québec City, Québec.